IMAGINE THAT

Licensed exclusively to Imagine That Publishing Ltd
Tide Mill Way, Woodbridge, Suffolk, IP12 1AP, UK
www.imaginethat.com
Copyright © 2018 Imagine That Group Ltd
All rights reserved
0 2 4 6 8 9 7 5 3 1
Manufactured in China

Written by Oakley Graham
Illustrated by Emi Ordás

ISBN 978-1-78700-860-1

A catalogue record for this book is available from the British Library

Beowulf
The Brave

A retelling of the epic *Beowulf* poem

by Oakley Graham

Illustrated by Emi Ordás

A long time ago, before you were born,
Lived a king with a golden drinking horn.
He ruled a cold land, that was peaceful and quiet,
Until a monster called Grendel started a riot!

Grendel hated laughter and one day, at a feast,
The king and his men were attacked by the beast!
The people were terrified, the hall stood silent,
What hero could stop the monstrous tyrant?

Then up stood Beowulf, Beowulf the Brave,
He feared no creature who lived in a cave!
His battles with monsters were legendary,
Remembered in song to make people feel merry.

No swords or spears could defeat the foul creature,
As magic protected its hideous features.
Grendel was stronger than an army of men,
The king's soldiers were scared to fight him again.

Beowulf swore to get rid of this horror,
And a banquet was held in the warrior's honour.
There was music and singing in the great hall,
Drinking and eating and even a brawl!

Under the light of a silvery moon,
Grendel charged into the great hall room.
Standing ten feet tall, he had come to fight,
And attacked the king's men with all his might!

The warriors tried to face the monster's attack,
But the fearsome beast just pushed them back.
All Beowulf's comrades and all the king's men,
Were soundly defeated by Grendel again!

Then up stood Beowulf, Beowulf the Brave,
To send the creature straight to his grave!
With no sword or armour, he launched an attack,
And knocked the foul monster down flat on his back!

Though Grendel had beaten all the king's men,
Beowulf attacked him again and again.
He fought the fierce monster, who tried to take flight,
But Grendel lay fatally wounded that night.

News of Grendel's demise was greeted with joy,
Except by his mother who mourned for her boy.
Now Grendel's mother was out for revenge,
And attacked one of Beowulf's very best friends.

So upset was Beowulf that his friend had been slain,
To destroy this new monster became his new aim.
He followed her tracks to her watery lair,
And with a giant's sword, he defeated her there.

Then home went Beowulf, Beowulf the Brave,
Across the sea on the ocean waves.
About his battles, the whole kingdom did sing,
And Beowulf was crowned as their new hero king!

Beowulf ruled peacefully for many a year,
Until someone disturbed a mound by a mere.
The mound concealed a great hoard of treasure,
That was a cruel fiery dragon's only pleasure!

Enraged that his secret hoard had been found,
The dragon took flight and scorched the ground.
Villages and towns, both near and far,
Were reduced to piles of ash and char.

'Help us please Beowulf, Beowulf the Brave!'
Was the plea from every man, woman and knave.
'Your battles with monsters are legendary,
Remembered in song to make us feel merry.'

So Beowulf got ready and put on his armour,
To battle the dragon and end all the drama.
He pounced on the beast and rode on its back,
And drew out his blade and began to attack!

Over the castle and mountains they flew,
Fighting each other as the stormy wind blew.
Beowulf slayed the dragon, he'd won the fight,
But in battle he'd suffered a deadly bite!

The kingdom was saved, the dragon defeated,
Beowulf's brave feats were never repeated.
His battles with monsters were legendary,
Remembered in song to make people feel merry.

Beowulf

Beowulf is the longest poem in Old English, the language spoken in Anglo-Saxon England before the Norman Conquest.

The story of Beowulf is set in Scandinavia way back in the 6th century. It is a story of good versus evil, with the Geatish warrior, Beowulf, saving his neighbours from a monster called Grendel, then defeating the monster's mother, and finally protecting his own kingdom from a dragon.

The original Beowulf poem is more than 3,000 lines long! The book you have just read is a shortened version and is written in modern English, but it still includes all of the main action!

The story of Beowulf was told by word-of-mouth for decades until it was finally written down around 1,000 years ago. Only a single copy of the manuscript survives. It is kept at the British Library in London.